I Didn't Do It!

A novel by

Paul Kropp

HIP-JR.

HIP Junior
Copyright © 2007 by Paul Kropp

LIBRARY AND ARCHIVES CANADA CATALOGUING IN PUBLICATION

Kropp, Paul, 1948–
    I didn't do it / Paul Kropp.

(HIP jr)
ISBN 978-1-897039-23-6

I. Title. II. Series.
PS8571.R772I45 2007   jC813'.54   C2007-901265-5

General editor: Paul Kropp
Text design and typesetting: Laura Brady
Illustrations drawn by: Kalle Malloy
Cover design: Robert Corrigan

2 3 4 5   14 13 12 11

Printed and bound in Canada

High Interest Publishing is an imprint of the
Chestnut Publishing Group

Tom didn't do any of the things they blamed on him. He didn't spray paint on the walls, or poison the hamster, or anything! But how could he prove that? And who was trying to get him into trouble?

CHAPTER 1

New Kid

I had my head down on my desk when the P.A. went off. I didn't much listen until I heard my name.

"Is Tom Foster in class?" It was from the office.

I lifted my head. By this time, all the kids were looking at me. You know that look – *Hey, the new kid's in trouble. That loser has to go to the office.* Their eyes were laughing at me.

Our teacher spoke back. "Yes, he's here."

"Send him to the office, please."

3

I groaned and got up from my desk. I'd only been in the city for a week, and already something had gone wrong. Even before I got to the door, I heard the whispers.

"Loser."

"Goof."

"Farmer!"

The last one was my nickname. You see, Farmer sounds a bit like Foster – my last name. I did move to the city from a farm. And I was stupid enough to say so on my very first day. In two seconds

Foster became Farmer. And then someone would add a "*hee-haw*" just to make it worse.

Real nice kids at this place. The guys don't want to know me. The girls treat me like I smell bad. And a couple of the girls keep giving me looks like they want me dead.

But maybe most junior high schools are like this. I've only been to two, so how would I know?

I got down to the office and had to sit on a bench. I waited, and waited. Then I looked for something to read. But there was nothing, not even a magazine. So I began to count the tiles on one wall. I must have looked like an idiot.

Then the principal came out. His name is Mr. Loney, so you can imagine what all the kids call him. Mr. Loney is a big guy. Maybe he was a gym teacher before he put on all the pounds. Now he looks like a Sumo wrestler – maybe six feet tall and six feet around.

"Tom," he said to me. "Would you come into my office?"

I got up and followed him. When I was inside,

he closed the door. That's when I knew it was bad news. The principal never closes the door on you unless it's bad.

"Yeah?" I said, but that sounded lousy. So I fixed it and said, "Yes."

"Please sit down," he said.

Now I really knew I was in trouble. A little trouble, they make you stand up to chew you out. A lot of trouble, they make you sit down.

Anyhow, I got the hard wooden chair. Mr. Loney sat in one of those cushy office chairs that lean way back.

"Tom, is there anything you want to tell me?" Mr. Loney began.

I hate that. A principal says *Is there anything you want to tell me* only when he thinks you did something. He wants you to confess. But confess to what? I hadn't done anything.

"No, sir," I replied. I thought it would be good to add the "sir." Maybe it would help.

"Are you not happy with our school?" Mr. Loney asked.

"Well, uh . . . ," I began.

The truth was simple. No, I wasn't happy. The kids at this place were all rich and a lot of them were stuck-up. They had all known each other since they were, like, two. And they had treated me like a real jerk.

But I couldn't say all that. Mr. Loney wasn't really looking for the truth. He was fishing for something.

"I've only been here a week," I said, thinking hard. "And my teachers are pretty good, I think . . ." Then I really put my brain in gear. "And the school is . . . very clean."

Boy, that seemed like a stupid thing to say. But I said it. That's what popped into my head and came out of my mouth.

"Clean?" Mr. Loney repeated.

"Yes," I told him. "It's cleaner than my old school."

This was true. My old school was out in the middle of a corn field. The little kids were always bringing in mud. But my old school had really good teachers. And I had friends there, guys I could count on. Even riding the school bus was kind of fun. But then we moved to the city – and it's all gone downhill.

"Well, Tom, let me get to the point," Mr. Loney said. "Do you remember when you went to the washroom today?"

"Yes." Of course I remembered. I had to wait until after this big, long lesson. And then some kid called me a dork when I left the classroom.

"Did anything happen in the washroom, Tom?"

I should have laughed. I mean, what did he think happens in a washroom? Did I need to tell him about it with all sorts of details?

"Meaning what?" I asked.

"Did you see anything? Did you notice anything on the walls?"

"No," I told him. I didn't even look at the walls. I mean, I was in a hurry!

"Nothing?" Mr. Loney asked.

"Nothing."

"No words on the walls? Nothing like that?"

"I wasn't really looking at the walls, sir," I told him.

Mr. Loney leaned back in his big chair. He looked hard at me. He seemed to be thinking about something. Then he sighed and sat forward.

"It would be better if you'd just admit it," he said. His voice was louder.

"Admit what?"

"That you did it!" He leaned in toward me.

"Did what?"

"You know what you did!" he said. Now Mr. Loney was almost shouting.

"I don't!" I said. My voice was starting to get shaky. When I was little, I would burst out crying. Now I don't do that any more, but sometimes I wish I could.

Mr. Loney sat back in his chair. He stared at me. I looked at him for a while, and then looked off at one wall. I could hear the clock ticking on the wall. We must have sat for five minutes in dead silence.

"When I get the proof, it will be worse for you," Mr. Loney told me.

"Proof of what?"

Mr. Loney sighed again. Then he shook his head and gave me a final order. "Go back to class, Tom, and think it over."

CHAPTER 2

Poison and Paint

I didn't have much time to think when I got back to class. Even before I got there, I could hear Mr. T's voice from the hall.

Mr. T was our homeroom teacher. He did some language arts teaching, too. But mostly he taught science. Mr. T is an awesome science teacher.

He is also an awesome guy. The kids call him Mr. T because he looks like that big guy on the old TV show – big, black, with lots of gold chains. Most of the time, Mr. T just smiles like crazy. He has a couple of gold teeth that are really cool. But when Mr. T gets mad . . . well, you can feel the earth shake.

I sure felt the door shake when he hit the wall with his fist.

"Who could do this?" he yelled. His voice has this big boom to it. "Who . . . could do . . . something like this?"

I opened the door and looked inside. All the kids seemed to be frozen in their desks. Mr. T was walking back and forth at the front of the room. I could see a hole in the wall where he had smashed it with his fist.

"Who?" he yelled. "What kind of person?"

I stepped into the room, closed the door and slipped into my desk.

Then there was silence. After a teacher gets really mad, there's an awful silence. Kids won't look at each other. No one wants to blame anyone else. No one wants to be blamed himself. You can only hear kids breathing and computer fans humming.

Then I heard something else. One of the kids

was crying. It was a guy I didn't really know. He was crying very quietly. But I knew the other guys would never let him forget it.

I wrote a quick note on a piece of paper. *What happened?* Then I passed it to the kid beside me.

Mr. T began shouting again. It took five minutes for the paper to come back to me. *Harry's dead. Poison.*

This was a shocker. Harry was the class hamster. He was part of a little class zoo that Mr. T kept in the room. We had a snake, a parakeet, a couple of fish, a big lizard and a small lizard. We also had a hamster . . . named Harry.

I looked over at the hamster cage. Harry wasn't moving.

I wondered if it really was poison. I mean, hamsters die of old age, just like people. But Mr. T wouldn't be yelling if Harry died of old age. Somebody had done something to kill Harry.

Who? What? This whole day didn't make any sense.

Mr. T stopped yelling at last. Nobody came

forward and said they killed the hamster. Mr. T kept staring, and nobody dared to say a word. After another twenty minutes, Mr. T was done. The class had to do worksheets for the rest of the morning. Talk about boring.

I still didn't know why Mr. T blamed us. How did he even know it was poison? And why our class? He taught all the science classes. There were even night classes in our school. I mean, it could have been anybody.

It wasn't until lunch time that I found out more.

Mr. T let us out of the room so we could get our lunches. We still had to go back and eat in our homeroom, but it gave us five minutes to talk.

So I turned to the guy at the next locker. His name was Jon. That was short for Jonathan Findlay III, or something like that, and he was a jock. He played all the sports in the school. A lot of kids looked up to him, and not just because he was tall. A lot of the "in" kids, like Jon, didn't talk to me. They treated me like I was some bug on the floor.

But Jon was okay. Not friendly, but okay.

"Why did Mr. T blame us?" I asked him.

"No good reason," Jon told me. "The hamster was okay last night, I guess."

"Was it poison?"

"Nobody knows," Jon replied. "Mr. T is going to have the hamster food tested. He says it smells funny, so that's where the poison thing came in."

So then I blurted out the big question. I mean, there was no reason for Jon to tell me. Even if he knew, there was no reason for him to speak to me. But I still had to ask.

"So who did it?"

"Don't know," he said, shutting his locker. "A couple of the girls blame you, Farmer. They say it's all gone rotten since you moved to town."

"Me?"

"Yeah," he told me. I had to look up at him. "They say you used spray paint in the washroom, too. That's the rumour."

"What spray paint?"

Jon just shook his head.

"Look, people don't know me," I said. "I'm not a bad guy, really. I'd never poison a hamster. I mean, that's pretty low. And spray paint? That's just stupid."

"Agreed," Jon replied. Then he turned to head off to volleyball practice.

I opened the lock on my locker. I reached up on the shelf to get my lunch. And then something fell out of my locker. It hit the floor with a metal *clang* and then rolled down the hall.

I turned to see what had fallen out. Jon turned to check out the noise. And Mr. T looked out from the classroom.

All three of us saw the same thing. A can of spray paint went rolling from my locker, down the hall.

CHAPTER 3

I Didn't Do It

So what could I say? The color of the spray paint was the same color as the one used in the washroom. It had been opened and used by someone. If it had my fingerprints, they could have sent me to jail.

But I had never seen the paint before. That's what I told Mr. T. That's what I told the principal. That's what I told my mother when they called her to take me home.

"You got off easy," my mom said as she drove.

"The school could have called the police. Then you'd be charged."

"I didn't do it," I told her. I must have said the same thing a dozen times. *I didn't do it.*

"Look, we all know you're unhappy with the move," my mom went on. "You didn't need spray paint to make that clear."

"I didn't do it," I said. That would be number fourteen.

"But we had no choice in the move, Tom. It was a big step up for your dad to come to head office. You know that. We know you didn't want to move, but give it a chance. Just don't act out."

My mom uses words like that – act out. She's always reading books on how to be a better parent. I think she keeps up with all the latest stuff. And maybe for my little sister, it works. For me, it makes me want to puke.

In my mind, I kept running over what had happened at lunch. Of course Mr. T sent me to the office. He sent Jon as a witness, and Jon took the can of paint. Old Mr. Loney went through the roof,

and then he called my mom. From all the talk later on, I found out why I was blamed. Someone used black spray paint on the girls' bathroom mirror. It happened about the same time as I went to the boys' bathroom. The funny thing was what was written with the spray can of paint: Farmer Freaks. That's the weird part. Even if I wanted to do something like that, why would I go to the girls' john? And why would I spray my own name on the wall? I mean, that's just stupid.

I may not be real smart, but I'm not *that* stupid.

When we got home, my mom and I walked in silence to the house. We got into the kitchen and I plunked into a chair.

"Did you ever think, Mom, that I was set up?" I asked her.

"What?"

"Set up," I repeated. "Somebody doesn't like me, so they set me up to look bad. Maybe somebody planted the spray paint in my locker."

"But why?" my mom asked. "You've only been here a week. How could you make an enemy like that so fast?" She stopped and looked at me. "Tom, tell me honestly. Did you do something to get on some kid's bad side?"

I shook my head. "I don't even *know* these kids. They're stuck-up. They don't talk to me, or hang with me. As far as they care, I don't even exist."

"Nice," Mom said.

"But true."

And that was the end of our talk.

That night, I sent an e-mail to one of my

buddies back home. Funny, I still think of our old house as "back home." This new house is just a place we live in – like, for now. My e-mail was pretty sad, when I read it over. But it was true, too.

From: tbones@lifeline.com
To: bradboy@internet.net

Hey, Brad, how's stuff? Things here are the pits. Got a two-day suspension today. Somebody used spray paint in the bathroom. Put my name up on the wall. Then put the paint can in my locker. Principal is so dumb he thinks I did it. And my homeroom teacher thinks I killed a hamster.

Good news – nobody called the cops. More good news – I didn't do it.

Life goes on. No friends. No TV (my mom is mad). No life.

Say hi to all my friends. Tell them I miss them – no guff. Tell them the big city isn't all it's cracked up to be. Hey, maybe my dad will get fired and then I can go home. See? There's always hope.

My old buddy got back to me real quick.

From: bradboy@internet.net
To: tbones@lifeline.com

Sounds bad, Tom. Never thought of you as a guy who'd murder a hamster. And a paint

can? You can't even handle a paint brush. I
think the city is getting to you!

So I got back to him, just as quick.

From: tbones@lifeline.com
To: bradboy@internet.net

Hey, I didn't do it. I'm innocent!

I like that word *innocent*. It's better than "not guilty." It sounds like you never did anything at all. Innocent until proven guilty, that's what the law says. And I wasn't guilty. The whole world *thought* I was guilty, but I wasn't.

I lay back on my bed and looked around my bedroom. It was ugly. We had moved right after my dad got the new job. This was the first house we looked at. My parents liked it right away. They said it was a good house, in a good neighborhood, with a good school.

Ha! The neighborhood is full of stuck-up rich

kids. The school principal thinks that I'm a wacko. And the house has water in the basement and bad paint. We moved so fast there was no time to repaint the walls. That's why my room is still pink. Pink! I hate it! My bedroom looks like some princess used to live here. Yecch!

CHAPTER 4

Loner?

I got to go back to school on Thursday. You can imagine the looks. Before, the kids looked at me like I was an insect. Now it was worse. They looked at me like I was some kind of dead skunk. A *rotting* dead skunk. Road kill!

I acted like I didn't care. What else could I do? There was no sense sucking up to a bunch of kids who hated me. In their eyes, I was guilty. In the principal's eyes, I was guilty. Only Mr. T seemed to give me a break.

He asked me to stay behind at lunch time. I thought he was going to let me have it. I thought I'd be blamed for the hamster. But I was wrong.

"Tom," he began. Mr. T is so big that he kind of towers over a guy. "I'm sorry about the other day."

"I didn't do it," I told him. I wasn't even sure what the "it" was.

"Not the spray paint," he replied. "The paint in your locker doesn't mean a thing. Those school locks are so bad that I can open half of them in two seconds flat."

"Right," I said, smiling for the first time. "And why would I even keep the can of paint? I mean, that's just dumb."

Mr. T nodded. "Listen, Tom, I didn't ask you to stay behind to talk about that. I wanted to talk to you about the hamster."

"Harry?"

"Yes," Mr. T said. "I kind of went nuts when he died. I was blaming all the kids and, really, it's nobody's fault. There was no poison. He just died, maybe from old age. He was three years old, and that's about as old as a hamster can get."

"I guess you were upset," I said.

"I guess I was," he replied. "I told the rest of the class about my mistake the other day. So I figured I should clue you in."

"Thanks."

"And by the way," he went on, "I don't think you sprayed the bathroom, in case you want to know. You strike me as a pretty decent kid."

"Thanks," I said. I was even blushing.

"But you don't seem too happy around here," Mr. T went on. "This school isn't a bad place, you know. Why not try to fit in?"

"Fit in?"

"Yeah, fit in. Join a club. Go out for a sport. Do something to meet some of the other kids. I tell you, Tom, there are times in my life I've been real lonely. And it's no fun."

"I'm not lonely," I said. That was a lie, but it's what I said.

Mr. T just looked at me. He has big eyes that sort of bug out of his head. When he looks at you,

you'd think he's looking right through you.

"Really, I'm not," I said.

Mr. T sighed, then told me to go have some lunch.

I had lunch by myself, of course. Nobody else would sit with me. So I unpacked my sandwich and ate, reading a comic book. I kept thinking about what Mr. T had said. Did I have a chip on my shoulder? Did I really like being a loner?

At my old school, in the country, I always had friends. I rode on the school bus with a bunch of guys I liked. At lunch, I played soccer and kickball and broomball with lots of guys. And then I had my close friends – Brad and Steve and maybe Rachel on the farm nearby. I wasn't a loner.

But now? It was like my whole life had gone into a tailspin when we moved. And now I had an enemy. Maybe a bunch of enemies. Somebody really did set me up. But who?

"Hey, Farmer," somebody called.

I looked up. It was a kid called Kareem. He was a tall Asian kid, kind of good looking. He looked

like a news guy on the CBC.

"Nice shirt. Is that what they wear back on the farm?"

A bunch of other kids laughed, then they went running off.

I turned red in the face. I was mad, of course. But what really made me mad was how slow I was. Why didn't I have a quick come-back? Why didn't I say, *sure, we use this for washing pigs like you!* But I always came up with stuff like that too late.

Later, a group of girls passed by. They were pointing at me and laughing. I acted like I couldn't hear them. Marcie and her friends were the *really* stuck-up girls, the rich ones who went skiing every weekend. In the summer, they rode horses. At Christmas, they went on pricey holidays. They lived in some other world.

Except, we were all in the same school. We were all stuck here together.

And I hated it.

On Friday, the day ended with science class. I was glad the week was over. Nothing good had happened. But at least I wasn't in jail. By now, I was getting used to kids staring at me, pointing and laughing. I got used to being called Farmer. That's just how it was.

In science class, our group was busy cutting up a worm. Mr. T put us in groups because no one wanted to be in mine. So I was in a group with Jon and Kareem. Jon cut up the worm. Kareem took the lab notes. I watched.

I kept watching until I got kind of sick. Maybe other guys can look at worm guts, but it doesn't work for me. Ugh.

"Hey, Farmer, you're looking kind of green," Jon said.

"What's the matter? Never saw worm guts on the farm?" Kareem asked.

I didn't say anything back. I just raised my hand and asked to be excused. When I made it to the bathroom, I threw up. Maybe it was the worm. Maybe it was something in my lunch. But I was really sick to my stomach.

I cleaned myself up and got ready to go back.

When I got back to my group, most of the work was done. The worm was cut in pieces. The worm pieces were all spread out. And Kareem had all the drawing done.

"You get clean-up," Kareem said. "Since you didn't do any work."

"Thanks," I said.

"Fair is fair," he told me.

"Right," I replied.

Just at that moment, the fire alarm went off. It seemed like a funny time for a fire drill. I mean,

Friday afternoon just before the bell? But there it was – *clang, clang, clang.*

"Stop your work," Mr. T shouted. "Get ready to go."

In a few seconds, we were lined up at the door. Another stupid fire drill, I thought. But then I saw smoke rolling under the door.

CHAPTER 5

Fire!

All those years of fire drills . . . and now a real fire. The smoke was dark and heavy. It rolled along the floor as we lined up.

"Okay, no panic," said Mr. T. "But let's move."

A couple of kids were coughing. A few kids were having a hard time breathing. But not me.

I was in a cold sweat. Ten minutes ago, I was throwing up in the john. And now, a fire. Put two and two together and you get . . . me.

We got outside pretty fast. So did the rest of the

school. In less than a minute, there were five hundred of us on the lawn and in the parking lot.

I could hear the fire engines before I saw them. Then, two minutes later, five trucks pulled up all at once. The firefighters were all ready to go. They were dressed in those heavy coveralls. Each of them had a breathing pack and an ax. From all that, you'd think the school was about to burn down.

The firefighters jumped off the trucks and ran into the school.

From outside, the rest of us just watched. There was a little smoke, but no fire. We could hear the sirens and the truck engines.

Nobody even talked much.

Five minutes later, the firefighters came out. One of them had a trash can. The trash can was soaked with water and foam. The firefighter shook his head, then tossed the garbage on the ground.

"That's it?" Jon said.

"A paper fire," Kareem told him.

And then they both began to laugh. The whole

school had to come outside because of a dumb fire in a trash can.

By now, the other kids were laughing, too. The fire had been scary at first, but now it was just a joke. At least, it was a joke for them.

The firefighters set up a big fan to get the smoke out of the school. A few minutes later, Mr. Loney came around with a loudspeaker. He told us that he was closing school early because of the fire. We were to go inside, get our books and head for home.

I knew that Kareem had grabbed our lab notes. If the cut-up worm got lost, that was the least of my worries. My worries were huge.

Mr. Loney grabbed me as I headed into the school. Mr. T was with him.

"Tom, is there anything you want to tell us?" Mr. Loney asked.

"Nope," I said.

"It will be easier for you," Mr. T added. "The joke's over. You might as well tell us what you did."

"I didn't do a thing," I told them. It seemed like

I'd been saying that all week.

They just stared at me.

I looked back at the two of them. "I didn't set the fire. Why would I? I don't even have matches."

Mr. Loney grabbed my arm. "We're going to find out who did this," he said.

I pulled my arm away from his hand. "Good. Then you'll see I had nothing to do with it."

*   *   *

Oh, it's easy to talk tough. It's easy to act like I wasn't scared. But inside I was shaking. Twice in one week! Each time I had gone off to the john, something had gone wrong. First the spray paint. Now the fire.

And somebody was trying to pin all of this on me.

I couldn't tell my parents. I just said there had been a trash fire and we were sent home early. That was enough. No sense getting them worried too.

But things couldn't go on like this. Sooner or

later, I'd get nailed for something. Then Mr. Loney would hang the spray paint and the fire on me, too. I might be looking at jail time, or a group home.

But what could I do? This wasn't like a TV show. I couldn't just phone CSI and say "help." I had no friends, no one on my side. I couldn't even tell my parents. I was on my own.

From: tbones@lifeline.com
To: bradboy@internet.net

Do I ever wish you were here, buddy. Today there was a fire at the school. On Monday, I'm gonna get blamed for it. These guys have got me pegged as a troublemaker. Me, your old buddy! The last time I made trouble was when we got in that fight back in grade four. Remember?

I'm sure somebody is setting me up. Don't know who. Don't know why. But somebody has it in for me. If I can figure out the who and the why, maybe I'll beat this. If not, please come visit me in jail. I'll be lonely.

My parents put me to work for the weekend. My mom got tired of hearing me complain about my room. "Pink," she'd say, "what's wrong with pink?" So on Friday, she let me have it. "No more complaints. You don't like pink, paint the room yourself." Then she drove me to the paint store and I picked a decent blue paint.

I had to spend one day getting the room ready. First I moved all the stuff in the room. Then I had to fill all the nail holes in the wall. And then I had to put tape around all the windows and the door frames. I mean, it takes longer to get ready than it does to paint!

But I had a bit of good luck in all that. When I was getting the closet ready, I found a photo. It was stuck between the wall and some moulding.

I pulled the photo out and looked at it. For a second, I thought it might be really old. But the picture was in color, and very new. There was even a date in the corner: a month before we moved in.

There were three girls in the photo. Two of them looked like girls in my class. The other girl was someone I didn't know. All three of them were in front of my house – I mean, my new house. On the back were six words: Marcie, Kenda & Tracy – friends forever.

And then it hit me. Sometimes an idea comes on so strong it almost knocks you over. That's what it felt like. Marcie, Kenda and Tracy – friends forever. But not friends of mine.

CHAPTER 6

"Get Lost, Farm Boy"

I looked hard at the photo. Yes, it was Marcie and Kenda from my class. Those were the two stuck-up girls who kept giving me nasty looks. I mean, none of the kids liked me. But only Marcie and Kenda were out-and-out *nasty*. Maybe they had something against me. Maybe they had turned the rest of the class against me.

Or not, I told myself, and I put the picture down. It all seemed crazy. I had nothing to do with this girl Tracy. I'd never seen her before in my life.

But still, the picture might mean something. And it might be a way to find out a little more.

That night, I got another e-mail from my buddy Brad.

From: bradboy@internet.net
To: tbones@lifeline.com

Hey, dude. You still the big city bad guy? Still getting blamed for all that stuff? Must be the pits. Back here, things are good. Played soccer the other day. Scored five goals. Can you believe it? Me!

BTW: The guys are all on your side. We'll go to court if we have to. Maybe tell the judge that you're a good guy. And if that doesn't work, we'll visit you in jail.

So I e-mailed back.

From: tbones@lifeline.com
To: bradboy@internet.net

*I'm still the bad guy. But I've got a hunch who
the real bad guys might be. And guess what?
They're girls. Stay tuned for more info.*

The next day, I painted my room. I also checked
with my mom. I asked her who owned the house
before us. She said it was a family named Rogers.
I asked if they had kids, but my mom didn't know.

"But it was a divorce sale," she told me.

"What does that mean?"

"It means that the parents were splitting up. They had to sell fast, so we got a really good price."

That gave me a brainwave. I even said it out loud. "I bet their kids didn't want to move."

"Maybe not," my mom said. "Who would want to leave a wonderful pink bedroom like yours?"

I groaned. At least my bedroom was now blue. And now I knew a little more. I was ready to take on Marcie and Kenda.

On Monday, I got pulled down to the office again. Mr. Loney kept asking me about the fire. He wanted to know why I had to go to the bathroom. And he kept asking me to confess.

I kept saying the same thing. "I didn't do it." That's the problem with adults. You can tell them the same thing, over and over, and they don't hear you.

In the end, there was nothing Mr. Loney could pin on me. I didn't set the fire, that's what I told him. I was innocent – and I really was.

Still, I was a little shaken when I got back to class. I had a hard time with the new whispers and jokes. My "Farmer" nickname was bad enough. But now I had lots more.

"Playing with matches, Farmer?"

"Oh, baby, light my fire."

"Should we call you Smokey?"

So I didn't take on the girls until Tuesday. By then, I was ready. I had the photo in my backpack and my plan ready to go.

I walked over to their lockers on the way to lunch. They were busy talking to each other, at least until I walked up.

Marcie looked at me first. "Uh-oh. I smell hay."

Kenda picked it up. "I smell cow poop."

Then Marcie, again. "Get lost, farm boy. Or do you want to set our lockers on fire, too?"

They both laughed. I just stood there and waited.

"I've got something you might want," I said.

That stopped them. But not for long. "You've got nothing *we* want, Farmer," Kenda said.

"It's a photo," I said, quietly. "You're both in it."

Now they were both looking at me. I took the

photo from my backpack but not so they could see
it.

"You know a girl named Tracy Rogers? Used to
live in my house?"

"Yeah?" Marcie replied. "So what?"

Now I had to smile. Two things made sense.
Tracy was their friend. I lived in Tracy's old house.
I had just painted Tracy's pink bedroom blue. Of
course, this didn't prove a thing. But it did give me
something to go on.

"She left this behind," I said. I handed them the picture. "I thought you might want it."

Of course, I had made a copy of the photo. I didn't know what to do with it, but I kept the copy.

Kenda grabbed the picture. "Where'd you get it?" she snapped.

I didn't answer the question. "What happened to Tracy?" I asked. "It says you're 'friends forever.'"

"She moved," Marcie blurted out. "Because of you, Farmer."

"Me?" I asked. I was surprised. Really, I was. "What did I do?"

"Your parents bought her house," Marcie went on. "They almost threw Tracy and her mom out on the street."

"My parents?"

"That's right, Farmer," Kenda said. "And we won't forget, not ever."

Marcie joined in. "We're going to make you wish you never moved here. You're going to wish you were still back on the farm, cleaning up cow poop."

Then they laughed and walked away. Neither of them bothered to say thanks for the picture. Maybe when you're that stuck-up, you don't ever say thanks.

CHAPTER 7

Setting the Trap

Now I was getting somewhere. I knew who my enemy was. I also knew why. Of course, the "why" seemed pretty dumb, but so what? I was still way ahead of where I was last week.

The problem, of course, was proof. I had no proof that Marcie and Kenda set me up. I couldn't prove that they used the spray paint. I couldn't prove that they set the fire. Without proof, I only had a hunch.

So I was stumped. I sent a long e-mail to my

buddy Brad. I explained the whole thing to him. He came back real quick.

From: bradboy@internet.net
To: tbones@lifeline.com

Sounds like a mess. How come the stuck-up girls blame you? Did you buy the house? No way. Sounds to me like they're more than a little crazy.

But how do you prove it to anybody else?

The answer is simple. Set a trap. Figure out some way to get them caught. Take a picture. Get a witness.

That's what they always do on TV. You're the bait. They're the fish. Now go catch them.

That seemed like a good idea. Or maybe a good start of an idea. The problem was – how could I set a trap?

It took me almost a week to come up with a plan. It was a really rough time. The girls kept staring daggers at me. I stared back at them. They knew that I knew. I knew that they knew I knew. It was tense.

But then I was ready.

The next Tuesday, Mr. T told us to get ready. We were going to cut up snakes the very next class. *Ugh*, I thought to myself. If a worm turned my stomach, a snake would be even worse. I'd be running to the bathroom in no time.

Then Marcie and Kenda would try something. No telling what, just something. And I knew I'd get blamed ... unless I got smart.

So on Wednesday, I was ready. Once again, Mr. T's science class was at the end of the day. All day long, the girls had been laughing and pointing at me. I knew they were planning something. But now I had a plan – and my mom's new camera.

When the snakes came out, I was ready. I stuck cotton up my nose, so high that no one could see. It was hard to breathe, but that was the plan. Who needs air when there's a dead snake on the work table?

I was with Jon and Kareem again. Neither of them had much to say to me. I think they blamed me for the fire, just like Mr. Loney. Not that it hurt them much. I mean, we just got sent home early. No big deal.

So the two of them were cutting up the snake. Jon did the cutting. Kareem pulled out the gooey bits. And I looked at the science book.

But then I raised my hand. "Mr. T," I said, "I feel kind of sick."

"Again?" he asked.

"Yeah, again," I told him. I thought my acting was pretty good. I almost felt sick just doing my fake. "Can I go to the bathroom?"

Mr. T grunted and I left. But I didn't go to the bathroom. I ducked around the corner of the hall. I hid in an empty classroom. And then I waited.

And waited. I checked my watch. Two minutes ... three ... four.

What was taking them so long? I thought. Was I wrong? Maybe it wasn't them after all. Maybe somebody else set me up.

But then I heard voices. I peeked out in the hall and saw them both: Marcie and Kenda. They were moving toward the front hall.

There was no way I could follow them. Kenda was looking all around, keeping watch.

So I thought fast. Quickly, I began moving the other way. The school is set up in a square, so the hallways would meet up. But maybe I could catch them by surprise.

I flew down the first hall. Then I peeked around the corner, and flew down the next. One more peek, and the third hall was clear. This time I went slowly, trying to be silent. They had to be near the office, right around the last corner. I got out the camera.

I got ready to jump around the corner. If they were doing something, I'd have my proof. If not, I'd look like a fool. My heart was racing as I turned on the camera. I set it to "burst" mode – five pictures in five seconds. Then I turned the corner.

Click!

Marcie had some lipstick. She was writing . . .

Click!

on Mr. Loney's picture. The lipstick was brown . . .
Click!

and looked like cow poop. Then Kenda turned
Click!

towards me. She froze and opened her mouth.
Click!

Marcie stopped writing and turned to look at
me.

Click!

That was the first burst of six shots. Now the

camera needed a couple of seconds to reset itself. I moved toward the girls, Marcie moved toward me. I think she was going to stab me with the lipstick. But then the camera went off again.

Click!

Marcie had the lipstick up in the air.

Click!

The lipstick was coming down. Fast.

Click!

I felt the lipstick hit my forehead. But the picture

Click!

was useless because it only got Marcie's arm.

Click!

Nor did the last picture get Kenda when she kicked me.

But the camera got enough. The flashes must have woken up Mr. Loney. When the tenth picture was done, he was standing in the hall.

The picture he saw was simple. Marcie was stabbing me with a lipstick. Kenda was kicking me. And Mr. Loney's picture said "Loney's . . ." I guess

Marcie never got to finish the second word.

"All right, that's enough," Mr. Loney said. It was his big principal voice. "All three of you – in my office."

CHAPTER 8

Picture Proof!

When we got into the office, the girls began to cry. I just sat there. I had the camera. Just hook the camera to a computer and – boom – there was the proof.

I smiled. The girls cried more. Mr. Loney began asking questions – about the spray paint and the fire. The girls lied . . . at least at first. They never did admit to the spray paint. But they did admit to the fire. "It was an accident," Marcie cried.

And Mr. Loney seemed to believe them. I wish

principals would be as tough on girls as they are on guys.

"And today?" Mr. Loney asked.

"It was just a joke," Kenda whined. "We didn't mean it."

And that was enough to turn my stomach. Her lies were worse than cutting up a dead snake.

"Tom, could I see the camera?"

I handed it over. Mr. Loney went through the pictures, one by one. When he was finished, he looked at me. "Could I borrow this for a while?" he asked. "I think the girls' parents should see this."

"Well, it's my mom's camera," I said. "I've got to take it back to her. Maybe we could just download them to a school computer."

And that's what I did. In ten minutes, I had burned two discs with all the pictures. One disc for Mr. Loney. One disc for me.

*   *   *

The girls didn't come back to school until the next week. Just like me, they got a couple of days at home. Unlike me, they got in big trouble with their parents.

In the meantime, the stories began to fly. All the girls were talking. Some of the guys heard some parts of the story. The girls all sided with Kenda and Marcie. But the guys, they had some questions.

It was Jon who came up to me at lunch on Friday. He had about five guys with him.

"So is it true?" he asked.

"Is what true?" I replied.

"That Marcie and Kenda got kicked out," Jon began. "That you caught them writing on Loney's picture."

"That's about it," I said with a shrug.

Then Kareem came in. "We heard there was a camera."

"A camera?" I asked. I tried to sound like it was a crazy idea.

"Yeah, somebody said there are pictures," Jon added. "Did you take pictures, or what?"

"Maybe I did, and maybe I didn't," I said. I was still being careful. These guys weren't my friends. There was no sense telling them the whole story. "But if those girls say one more nasty thing about me, I might have something to show you."

Jon smiled. "Hey, Farmer, that is cool!"

Kareem agreed. "Smart move, guy. Those two are a nasty pair. You hold on to those pictures and they'll never say a word."

I nodded. "Kind of what I thought," I said.

Kareem hit me on the back. "Hey, Farmer, you ever play soccer?"

"Once or twice," I told them. "Back down on the farm."

All of them laughed. Then Jon gave me a big, big smile. "Let's see if you country guys can really kick a ball."

The answer to that question was really simple. I e-mailed it to my friend Brad that night. I scored five goals – easy as pie. These city kids can't defend the net!

Three Feet Under

by PAUL KROPP

Scott and Rico find a map to long-lost treasure. There's $250,000 buried in Bolton's mine. But when the school bully steals their map and heads for the old mine, the race is on.

The Crash

by PAUL KROPP

A school bus slides off a cliff in a snowstorm. The bus driver is out cold. One of the guys is badly hurt. Can Craig, Rory and Lerch find help in time?

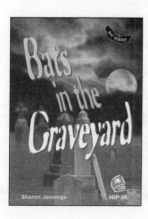

Bats in the Graveyard

by SHARON JENNINGS

Sam and Simon have to look after Simon's little sister on Halloween night. Soon the boys end up in a cemetery — spooked!

Paul Kropp is the author of more than fifty novels for young people. His work includes nine award-winning young adult novels, many high-interest novels, as well as books and stories for both adults and early readers.

Paul Kropp's best-known novels for young adults, *Moonkid and Liberty* and *Moonkid and Prometheus*, have been translated into many languages and have won awards around the world. His high-interest novels have sold nearly a million copies in Canada and the United States. For more information on Paul, visit his website at www.paulkropp.com.

For more information on HIP novels:

High Interest Publishing – Publishers of H·I·P Books
407 Wellesley Street East • Toronto, Ontario M4X 1H5
www.hip-books.com